Té para RUBY

Té para RUBY

Tea for RUBY

by/por
SARAH FERGUSON
THE DUCHESS OF YORK
DUQUESA DE YORK

illustrated by/ilustrado por
ROBIN PREISS GLASSER

A Paula Wiseman Book
Simon & Schuster Books for Young Readers
New York   London   Toronto   Sydney

To Beatrice and Eugenie—
you make my world complete
—S. F.

For Jacqueline Preiss Weitzman—
my sister, my partner, my friend
—R. P. G.

A Beatrice y Eugenie—
vosotras completáis mi mundo
—S. F.

Para Jacqueline Preiss Weitzman—
mi hermana, mi compañera, mi amiga
—R. P. G.

SIMON & SCHUSTER BOOKS FOR YOUNG READERS • An imprint of Simon & Schuster Children's
Publishing Division • 1230 Avenue of the Americas, New York, New York 10020 • Text copyright
© 2008 by Sarah Ferguson, The Duchess of York • Illustrations copyright © 2008 by Robin Preiss
Glasser • All rights reserved, including the right of reproduction in whole or in part in any form. Cheerios® is
a registered trademark of General Mills. • SIMON & SCHUSTER BOOKS FOR YOUNG READERS is a trademark of Simon
& Schuster, Inc. • Book design by Dan Potash • The text for this book is set in Fiddlestix. • The illustrations
for this book are rendered in ink, watercolor, and colored pencil. • Manufactured in the United States
of America • Library of Congress Cataloging-in-Publication Data • York, Sarah Mountbatten-Windsor,
Duchess of, 1959– • Tea for Ruby / Sarah Ferguson, The Duchess of York ; illustrated by Robin Preiss Glasser.
• p. cm. • "A Paula Wiseman book." • Summary: As Ruby tells everyone about her invitation for tea
with the Queen, family and friends remind her about how she should conduct herself.
• ISBN 978-1-4169-9417-6 • [1. Etiquette–Fiction. 2. Kings, queens, rulers, etc.–Fiction. 3. Afternoon
teas–Fiction.] I. Preiss-Glasser, Robin, ill. II. Title. • PZ7.Y823Te 2008 • [E]–dc22 • 2007045350

*Estás invitada
a tomar té con
la Reina
el domingo.*

*Favor de traer tus
mejores modales.*

You are invited
to have tea with
The Queen
on Sunday.

Please bring your very best manners.

"the Queen."

la Reina.

"The Queen."
la Reina.

"The Queën".

la Reina.

"I've been invited to have tea with the Queen!"

—¡Estoy invitada a tomar té con la Reina!

"I've been invited to have tea with the Queen!"

—¡Estoy invitada a tomar té con la Reina!

"Ruby, I hope you will
dress appropriately
when you have tea with . . . **The Queen**."

—Ruby, ojalá que te
vistas apropiadamente
cuando tomes té con . . . la Reina.

"I've been invited to have tea with the Queen!"

—¡Estoy invitada a tomar té con la Reina!

Only 6 items at a time in dressing rooms, please.

Sólo 6 artículos por vez en el probador, por favor.

"Ruby, I hope you will say 'please' and 'thank you' when you have tea with . . .

—Ruby, ojalá que digas "por favor" y "gracias" cuando tomes té con . . .

"The Queen"

la Reina.

oops

"I've been invited to have tea with the Queen!"

—¡Estoy invitada a tomar té con la Reina!

MR. ROY'S PUPPET FARM

"Ruby, I hope you won't talk when you shouldn't when you have tea with . . .

—Ruby, ojalá que no hables cuando no debes cuando tomes té con . . .

"The Queen."

la Reina.

The Queen.

la Reina.

"Ruby, I hope you won't talk with your mouth full and won't tip your chair back and will use your fork and napkin when you have tea with ...

—Ruby, ojalá que no hables con la boca llena y no hagas la silla para atrás y ojalá que uses el tenedor y la servilleta cuando tomes té con ...

The Queen

la Reina.

"Tomorrow I'm having
tea with the Queen!"

–¡Estoy invitada a tomar
té con la Reina mañana!

"Ruby, I hope you'll remember
to sit up straight when you
have tea with the Queen."

–Ruby, ojalá que te acuerdes
de sentarte derecha cuando
tomes té con la Reina.

Today's the day!

¡Hoy es el día!

"Let's hurry so we won't be late!"

—¡De prisa, para no llegar tarde!

Remember to chew with my mouth closed.
Masticar con la boca cerrada.

Remember not to speak with my mouth full.
No hablar con la boca llena.

Remember to say "please" and "thank you."
Decir "por favor" y "gracias."

Remember to welcome people.
Dar la bienvenida a la gente.

Remember to use my fork and napkin.
Usar el tenedor y la servilleta.

Remember not to interrupt.
No interrumpir.

Remember not to shout.
No gritar.

Remember to wait my turn.
Esperar mi turno.

Remember to sit up straight.
Sentarme derecha.

Remember not to talk when I shouldn't.
No hablar cuando no debo.

"GRANDMA?"

—¿ABUELITA?

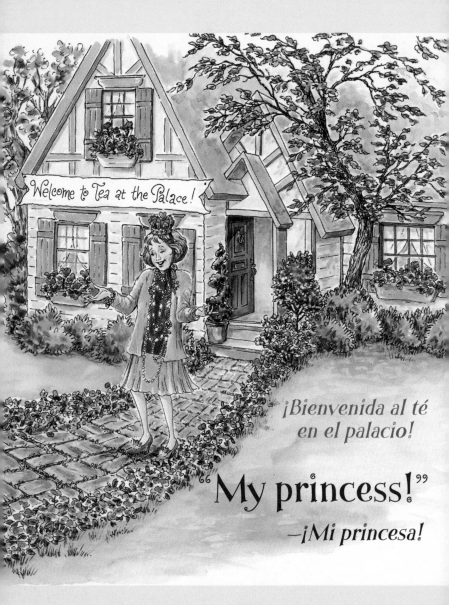

¡Bienvenida al té
en el palacio!

"My princess!"
—¡Mi princesa!

"May I offer
you more tea,
Princess Ruby?"

—¿Más té,
Princesa Ruby?

"Oh, yes,
please, Grandma.
Thank you."

—Ah, sí, por favor,
Abuelita. Gracias.

Dear Grandma,
Thank you so much
for inviting me to
tea. I tried to use
my very best manners.
The tarts were delicious
but my favorite thing
was just being with
you! I Love you,
Ruby

Querida Abuelita:
Muchísimas gracias por
invitarme al té. Traté de tener
lucir mis mejores modales.
¡Las tartas estuvieron deliciosas pero lo
que absolutamente me gustó más fue estar
contigo!
Te quiero,
Ruby